Winnie the Pooh
and the Honey Tree

PaRragon

Bath · New York · Singapore · Hong Kong · Cologne · Delhi · Melbourne

Winnie the Pooh lived in an enchanted forest under the name of Sanders, which means he had the name over the door and he lived under it. Now when Pooh heard his Pooh Coo Clock, he knew it was time for something.

"Think, think, think. Oh yes. Time for my stoutness exercise."

Pooh stood in front of his mirror and tried to touch his toes. "Up, down and touch the ground. Up, down and touch the ground …"

But instead of making him thin, the exercise made Pooh hungry. So he went to his cupboard, got down a honey jar and inspected his honey supply.

"Oh, bother. Empty again. Only the sticky part's left."

Pooh put his head in the jar and tried to get at the last bit of honey, when he heard a buzzing sound.

"That buzzing noise means something. And the only reason for making a buzzing noise that I know of is because you're a … a bee! And the only reason for being a bee is to make honey."

Pooh followed the bee outside to a nearby tree. High
in a hole near the top sat a beehive full of honey.
"And the only reason for making honey is so I can eat it."
So Pooh began to climb the honey tree.

He climbed and he climbed. And just as Pooh neared the beehive, the branch he was standing on broke and down went Pooh, into a very prickly bush below.

"Oh, bother."

Pooh brushed the prickles from his nose and decided to go ask Christopher Robin for help.

"Christopher Robin,
I was wondering if you had such
a thing as a balloon about you?"
Christopher Robin happened
to have just the thing. "But what do you
want a balloon for?"

"Honey. I shall fly like a bee, up to the
honey tree."

Pooh ran off to a very muddy place near the honey tree
and Christopher Robin followed. Pooh rolled around and
around until he was covered with mud from his nose
to his toes. Christopher Robin scratched his head and
wondered what Pooh was up to. "What are you supposed
to be, Pooh?"

"A little black rain cloud, of course. Now, would you aim me at the bees, please?" Christopher Robin handed Pooh the balloon and launched him into the air.

Pooh rose higher and higher toward the hole in the top of the honey tree. And while he hovered outside, a bee flew from the hive and landed on Pooh's nose.

"Christopher Robin, I think the bees suspect something. Maybe it would help with the deception if you would open your umbrella and say, "Tut, tut, it looks like rain.""

So Christopher Robin opened his umbrella and paced back and forth beneath it. "Tut, tut, it looks like rain!"

The little bee, however, was not fooled. He knew the difference between a rain cloud and a hungry Pooh Bear. So, he flew at Pooh and stung him directly on his softest spot.

"Oh!" Pooh swung left, then right, then quite by accident swung his very sore bottom into the hole in the tree.

"Oh dear. I'm stuck."

In no time, the bees inside the tree created a mighty force and they pushed Pooh out of the hole, sending him shooting across the sky. The balloon sputtered and Pooh came tumbling downward.

"Oh, bother. I think I shall come down now."

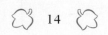

Pooh fell from the sky with the bees in hot pursuit.
Christopher Robin gently caught him and together they
ran to the muddy place and jumped in. Christopher Robin
opened his umbrella and they hid beneath it as the bees
buzzed past. The bees did not bother them any more
that day.

Once Pooh began thinking about honey, he just couldn't stop. So, he made his way to Rabbit's house for a light honey snack. "Hello, Rabbit!"

"Oh dear. Hello, Pooh Bear. What a surprise. Well, how about lunch?"

Pooh sat himself down at the table and tied a napkin around his neck. Rabbit knew perfectly well what Pooh was hungry for. He reluctantly pulled out a honey jar and offered it to Pooh.

"Thank you, Rabbit. Just a small helping, please."

Pooh helped himself to Rabbit's honey and he ate and he ate and he ate and he ate, until there was no honey left. Finally, in a very sticky voice, he excused himself.

"I must be going now. Goodbye, Rabbit."

Pooh thanked Rabbit and he turned to leave. But Pooh's tummy, full of honey, only got halfway out of Rabbit's small front door.

"Oh, bother. I'm stuck."

Rabbit pushed at Pooh's round bottom, but it was no use.

"Oh, dear. Oh, dear. There's only one thing to do. I'll get Christopher Robin." Rabbit hurried out of the side door to find his friend.

In a short time, Rabbit returned with Christopher Robin. "Cheer up, Pooh Bear. We'll get you out."

Christopher Robin took hold of Pooh and Rabbit took hold of Christopher Robin. And on the count of three, they pulled as hard as they could. But Pooh wouldn't budge.

"It's no use. I'm stuck."

Christopher Robin shook his head. "Pooh Bear, there's only one thing to do – wait for you to get thin again."

Nobody knew how long it would take Pooh to get thin, so poor Rabbit tried to make the best of the situation by decorating Pooh's bottom with a picture frame and some antlers.

"There. A hunting trophy. Ahh... I know what it needs." Rabbit then painted a face on Pooh's bottom. It tickled and Pooh wriggled. "Oh, Pooh. You messed up my moose."

And while Rabbit got along with Pooh's back end, his front end was visited by many friends, including Kanga and little Roo.

"Pooh, Roo has a little surprise for you." Roo handed Pooh a big bouquet of flowers. Pooh took a deep sniff.

"Honeysuckle. Thank you, Roo."

Day after day, night after lonely night, Pooh waited to get thin. And while he waited, who should pop up one night but his good friend Gopher. "I'm working the swing shift, sonny. But now it's time for my midnight snack."

Gopher opened his lunch box and inspected its contents, while Pooh looked on with a hungry 'feed me' sort of look. "Let's see here … summer squash, succotash, spiced custard … and honey."

Pooh brightened at the sound of his favourite word. "Honey? Could you spare a small smackerel?"

But before Pooh could attempt a taste, Rabbit whipped out of his side door and planted a large sign next to Pooh.

"Don't feed the bear!"

Poor Pooh. Gopher quickly went back to work and Pooh continued his long and very hungry wait.

And then, one morning when Rabbit was beginning to think that he might never be able to use his front door again, it happened. He leaned up against Pooh's bottom and …

"He boodged! Christopher Crabin! Eh, ah, Crostofer Raban. He bidged! He badged! He bodged! Today is the day!"

Almost everyone in the Hundred-Acre Wood came running to help. From inside his house, Rabbit pushed frantically on his end of Pooh, while outside everyone else pulled on the other end.

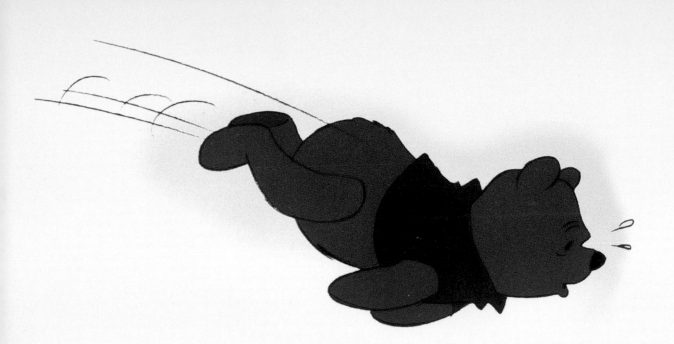

"Heave-ho! Heave-ho!" They tugged and they pushed and they pulled and they shoved with all their might, until suddenly, Pooh shot out of the hole and flew high overhead into the treetops, where he landed in the hole in the honey tree.

Christopher Robin called from down below. "Don't worry, Pooh. We'll get you out."

"No hurry. Take your time!"

For you see, Pooh had landed right in the middle of the beehive and some very yummy honey.

"Yum, yum. Bears love honey and I'm a Pooh Bear. Yum, yum, yum, yum. Time for something sweet."

Christopher Robin shook his head and grinned. "Silly old bear."

Winnie the Pooh
and a Day for Eeyore

One day, as Winnie the Pooh stood on the old wooden bridge that crossed the river that ran through the Hundred-Acre Wood, he dropped a fir cone into the water. Pooh watched it disappear then reappear on the other side of the bridge. "Now if I drop two cones, I wonder which will come out first?"

Well, as Pooh quite expected, the big one came out first and the little one came out last. And that was how Pooh invented the game called 'Pooh Sticks', even though he began with fir cones.

Not long after that, Pooh and Piglet, Rabbit and Roo were all playing Pooh Sticks together. Rabbit recited the rules.

"All right now. The first stick to pass all the way under the bridge wins. On your marks … get set … go!"

Pooh anxiously waited to see which stick would come out first. "I see your stick, Piglet! It's the grey one!"

But Pooh soon discovered that it wasn't a grey stick at all. It was Eeyore's tail. And if you find Eeyore's tail, you can be most assured of finding …

"Eeyore!"

"Don't pay any attention to me. Nobody ever does."

Now the problem was how to get Eeyore out of the water. Pooh offered a suggestion. "If we all threw stones and things into the river on one side of Eeyore, the stones would make waves and the waves would wash him to the other side." It was a most brilliant solution. And the others quite agreed. Pooh found a nice big boulder and rolled it onto the bridge. Rabbit, as usual, gave the instructions. "All right, Pooh, when I say 'now', you can drop it. One ... two ... NOW!"

Unfortunately, the boulder hit Eeyore in the softest spot of his tummy ... and ... he sank. Pooh shook his head as he watched his friend disappear.

"Oh, dear. Perhaps it wasn't such a very good idea." But just then, Piglet caught sight of Eeyore climbing up onto the riverbank. "Look! There he is!"

Of course, they all wanted to know how Eeyore had fallen in. Emptying the water from one ear, the old grey donkey explained. "I was thinking by the side of the river, minding my own business, when I received a loud bounce."

Before anyone could make a guess as to what that meant, a very bouncy Tigger came bouncing down the path and bowled over the unsuspecting Rabbit. "Hello, Rabbit!"

"Tigger, did you bounce Eeyore?"

"No, I didn't. Really. I, uh, I just had a cough, see? And besides, bouncing is what Tiggers do best!"

Rabbit nodded grimly. "Ah-ha! So, you did bounce Eeyore, eh, Tigger?"

"Some people have no sense of humour." And with that, . Tigger turned and bounced off down the path.

A very soggy Eeyore watched Tigger leave. "Why should Tigger care? Nobody else does."

And while his friends puzzled over his unusual behaviour, Eeyore followed the river back to his gloomy spot. Pooh ran after him.

"Eeyore, what's the matter? You seem so sad."

"Why should I be sad? It's my birthday. The happiest day of the year. Can't you see all the presents? The cake? The candles and the pink sugar frosting?"

Of course there were no presents, or cake, or candles, or pink sugar frosting.

"But don't worry about me, Pooh. Go and enjoy yourself."

Pooh felt very bad for Eeyore, so he hurried home as fast as he could to tell the others. When he arrived at his house, who should he find there but ...

"Piglet!"

"Hello, Pooh! I was trying to reach the knocker."

"Let me do it for you." Pooh lifted the knocker and rapped on the door.

"Piglet, I found out what's troubling poor Eeyore. It's his birthday and nobody has taken any notice of it."

Now you'll remember that Pooh is a bear of very little brain. "Well, Piglet, whoever lives here certainly takes a long time answering his door."

"But Pooh, isn't this your house?"

"Oh, so it is!" Pooh opened the door and they went inside.

"Piglet, I must get poor Eeyore a present of some sort."
Pooh went directly to his cabinet and got down a nice big
jar of honey. "This should do very well. What are you going
to give him, Piglet?"

"Perhaps I could give Eeyore a balloon. I have one at
home." Piglet trotted off in one direction to his house and
in the other direction went Pooh with his jar of honey towards
Eeyore's gloomy spot.

Pooh had only travelled a short distance when a little voice from deep inside his tummy spoke to him. "Now then, Pooh, time for a little something."

So Pooh had a little something and then he had a little more and a little more, until he had taken the last lick from the inside of the honey jar.

"Oh, bother. This jar seems to be missing something. Perhaps Owl can help."

At Owl's house, Pooh explained all about Eeyore's birthday. Owl nodded wisely. "What are you giving him, Pooh?"

"I'm giving him this useful pot to keep things in. And I was wondering if you could write something on it. My spelling is wobbly."

So Owl wrote on the pot: 'A Happy Birthday, With Love From Pooh'. Pooh thanked Owl and happily went on his way, while Owl flew off to tell Christopher Robin about Eeyore's birthday.

As Owl flew overhead, Piglet waved from down below, holding tight to the bright red balloon he was taking to Eeyore. "Hello, Owl! Many happy returns of Eeyore's… Ooff!" He ran straight into the trunk of a tree. Piglet and the balloon bounded up and down, up and down, until the balloon burst.

"Oh, dear. What shall I? How shall I? Well, perhaps Eeyore doesn't like balloons very much." Piglet sadly gathered up the flattened balloon and continued on his way.

It wasn't long until Piglet found Eeyore sitting under a tree. "Good afternoon, Eeyore."

"Good afternoon, Piglet. If it is a good afternoon, which I doubt."

Piglet handed Eeyore what was left of the balloon. "I'm very sorry. But when I was running to bring it, I fell down."

Eeyore looked at the balloon and smiled. "A birthday balloon? For me? And it's red. My favourite colour."

Just then, Pooh arrived. "I've brought you a little present, Eeyore. It's a useful pot, for putting things in."

"Like a balloon?" Eeyore picked up the balloon in his mouth, dropped it in the pot, then took it out again.

Pooh was very pleased with himself. "I'm glad I thought of giving you a useful pot to put things in"

Piglet grinned a big grin. "And I'm glad I thought of giving you something to put in a useful pot."

Later that day, Christopher Robin gathered everyone together to celebrate Eeyore's birthday and he brought along a cake covered with pink sugar frosting. Eeyore made a wish and blew out all the candles. Then Christopher Robin cut the cake and passed it around so that everyone had a piece.

Just then, a great 'Halloo' was heard over the celebration. Rabbit knew it could mean only one thing.

Sure enough, Tigger came bouncing along and knocked Rabbit to the ground. Christopher Robin giggled. "Hello, Tigger. We're having a party."

"A party? Oh, boy! Tiggers love parties! And cake!"

Rabbit glared at Tigger. "You've got a lot of nerve showing up here after what you did to Eeyore. I think Tigger should leave." But Christopher Robin had a better idea. "I think we all ought to play Pooh Sticks!"

So they gathered on the old wooden bridge and played the game for many contented hours. And Eeyore, who had never played it before, won more times than anybody else.

But poor Tigger won none at all. "Grrr…Tiggers don't like Pooh Sticks."

It was getting late and Rabbit decided that it was time for them all to be going home. Owl agreed. "Yes, quite right. Congratulations, Eeyore. It's been a delightful party."

As Tigger trudged sadly home, Eeyore caught up to him. "Tigger, I'd be happy to tell you my secret for winning at Pooh Sticks."

"You would?"

"It's very easy. You just have to let your stick drop in a 'twitch' sort of way."

Tigger laughed and bounced along after Eeyore. "Oh, yeah! I forgot to twitch! That was my problem!"

Then, just on the other side of the hill, where no one could see, Tigger bounced Eeyore, because that's what Tiggers do best. And Eeyore, with memories of a wonderful birthday, didn't seem to mind a bit.